A NOTE TO PARENTS

When your children are ready to "step into reading," giving them the right books—and lots of them—is as crucial as giving them the right food to eat. **Step into Reading Books** present exciting stories and information reinforced with lively, colorful illustrations that make learning to read fun, satisfying, and worthwhile. They are priced so that acquiring an entire library of them is affordable. And they are beginning readers with an important difference—they're written on four levels.

Step 1 Books, with their very large type and extremely simple vocabulary, have been created for the very youngest readers. **Step 2 Books** are both longer and slightly more difficult. **Step 3 Books,** written to mid-second-grade reading levels, are for the child who has acquired even greater reading skills. **Step 4 Books** offer exciting nonfiction for the increasingly proficient reader.

Children develop at different ages. **Step into Reading Books,** with their four levels of reading, are designed to help children become good—and interested—readers *faster*. The grade levels assigned to the four steps—preschool through grade 1 for Step 1, grades 1 through 3 for Step 2, grades 2 and 3 for Step 3, and grades 2 through 4 for Step 4—are intended only as guides. Some children move through all four steps very rapidly; others climb the steps over a period of several years. These books will help your child "step into reading" in style!

For dinosaur hunter George Kleuser

Text copyright © 1989 by Kate McMullan. Illustrations copyright © 1989 by John R. Jones. All rights reserved under International and Pan-American Copyright Conventions. Published in the United States by Random House, Inc., New York, and simultaneously in Canada by Random House of Canada Limited, Toronto.

Library of Congress Cataloging-in-Publication Data:
McMullan, Kate. Dinosaur hunters. (Step into reading. A Step 4 book) SUMMARY: Describes the work scientists do to find out more about these huge prehistoric animals. 1. Paleontology–Juvenile literature. 2. Dinosaurs–Juvenile literature. [1. Dinosaurs] I. Jones, John, 1935–   ill. II. Title. III. Series: Step into reading. Step 4 book.   QE714.5.M37   1989   567.9′1   88-30742
ISBN: 0-394-81150-X (pbk.); 0-394-91150-4 (lib. bdg.)

Manufactured in the United States of America   10

STEP INTO READING is a trademark of Random House, Inc.

Step into Reading

DINOSAUR HUNTERS

By Kate McMullan
Illustrated by John R. Jones

A Step 4 Book

Random House 🏠 New York

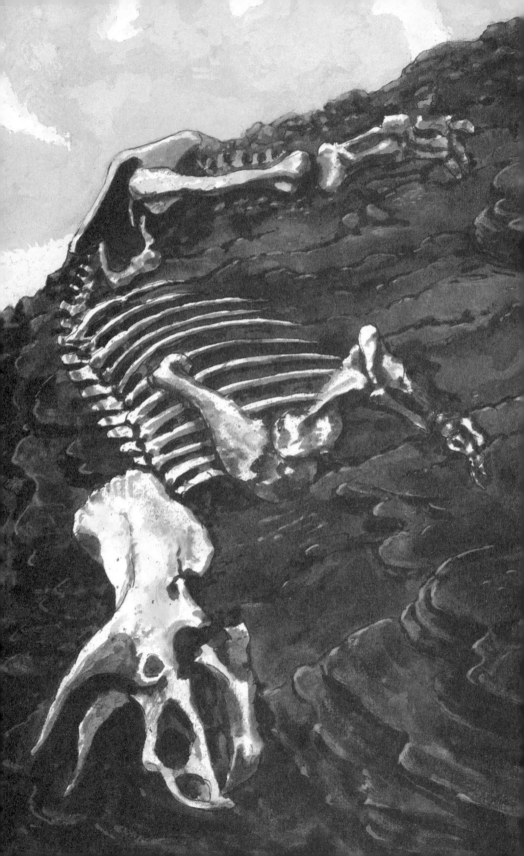

1

A Monster in Stone

Jim Jensen is a famous dinosaur hunter. He has been hunting dinosaurs for years and years. Once he discovered a dinosaur with a third eye in the middle of its forehead. Another time he discovered the biggest dinosaur ever. He is the best dinosaur hunter there is. That's why he's called Dinosaur Jim.

Of course, dinosaurs don't live on earth anymore. The last ones disappeared about sixty-five million years ago. So how can Dinosaur Jim hunt dinosaurs if there aren't any around?

To find out, imagine it is 140 million years ago. The oceans are warm and shallow. The weather is always sunny and dry. Lush green ferns and palmlike trees grow everywhere. Dinosaurs of all shapes and sizes roam the earth.

Some of the dinosaurs are no bigger than a chicken. Others are taller than a six-story building. Some have horns and spikes. Others have duck bills and bird feet. There are no people yet. It is the middle of the Mesozoic (mez-uh-zo-ik) Era. It is the age of reptiles.

Picture a huge Brontosaurus (bron-tuh-SAWR-us) walking to a lake. Its footsteps echo like thunder through the forest. This Brontosaurus is old and weak. It takes a last drink from the lake. Then it falls on its side in the mud. It is dead.

In time the soft flesh of the dead Brontosaurus rots away. But the hard bones sink deep into the mud. The mud protects the bones. They do not rot away.

For millions of years the bones lie under the ground. Rain falls. It seeps down through the ground, dissolving minerals in the rocks. The rainwater carries the minerals along as it trickles down, down to the bones.

Like all bones, the Brontosaurus bones are filled with holes too small to see. The rainwater seeps into these holes. The water evaporates. But the minerals in the water stay and harden in the bones. Little by little what once was bone turns to stone. The bones of the Brontosaurus are now stone fossils.

WATER DEPOSITS MINERALS IN THE BONE.

THE BONE TURNS INTO A STONE FOSSIL.

Earthquakes rattle these fossil bones around. Volcanoes erupt and bury the bones under layers of lava. Glaciers drag tons of ice and snow over the bones. Oceans flow over the land. Their currents lay tons of sand and broken shells over the bones. The weight presses on the mud around the bones. Slowly the weight turns the mud around the bones to stone too.

Millions more years pass. The earth shifts. Mountains rise. The Brontosaurus bones are pushed up. A few of the bones are sticking out of a cliff. Sunlight is shining on the Brontosaurus once again.

It is fossilized bones like these that Dinosaur Jim is hunting. For Dinosaur Jim is a paleontologist (pay-lee-un-TOL-uh-jist). He is a scientist who studies plants and animals from the past. When Dinosaur Jim finds a fossil, he tries to figure out what that fossil can tell him.

Can it tell him what the dinosaur looked like? How fast it ran? What it ate? Dinosaur Jim wants to find out as much as he can about the world of dinosaurs. And fossils are his best clues!

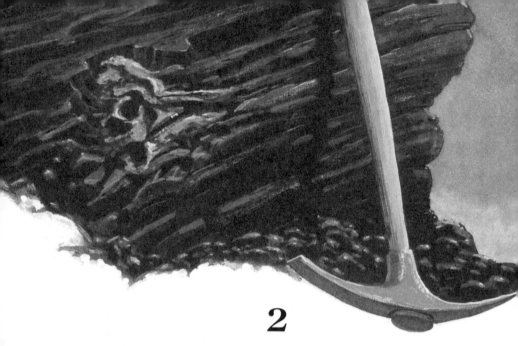

2

The Giant Tooth Mystery

People have been finding dinosaur fossils for thousands of years. They have found them in cliffs and along riverbanks. They have found them while digging for gold and silver. The name *fossil* comes from Latin. It means "to dig." And that is usually how people found them!

Until about two hundred years ago people did not know what these big bones were. That's because they did not know dinosaurs had ever existed. They thought the dinosaur

bones must have come from hippos or elephants or other large creatures. They never
suspected that creatures—very different creatures from the animals they knew—had once
lived on earth.

But some of the bones people found were
huge. They were too big to have come from an
elephant or a hippo. These huge bones made
some people believe that giants and ogres
really did exist. Native Americans thought

that the bones were skeletons of giant serpents. In China the big bones were said to be dragon bones. They were ground into powders. People mixed the bone powder into a potion and drank it. They believed the dragon bones would make them powerful.

About four hundred years ago a man named Bernard Palissy wrote about fossils. He was a French pottery maker. He wrote that fossils were the remains of living creatures. This was not a new idea. But Palissy wrote something else. He wrote that these creatures no longer lived on earth. All of them had died, he said. They were extinct.

Extinct? That meant different animals had once lived on earth and had completely disappeared! No one had ever said such a thing before!

Did Palissy become famous for his discovery? No! People were frightened by his ideas. And Palissy was put in prison.

But as time went on, people grew more interested in science. They became more open to new ideas about the world and what it had been like millions of years ago.

Then in 1822 something important happened. An English fossil collector, Mary Ann Mantell, was walking down a road one day. The road was being repaired. There were broken-up rocks all around. In the rocks Mary Ann saw what looked like a very large tooth. She picked it up. The tooth felt like stone. It was a fossil.

Mary Ann took the big stone tooth home and showed it to her husband, Gideon. He was a doctor and a scientist. Together they examined the tooth. It was flat and smooth. The tooth was also worn down the way teeth get after years of chewing food. It looked something like an elephant's tooth. But it couldn't be. Gideon knew that because he knew a lot about rocks. He knew that the rock around the tooth was very old. And he knew that no fossils of elephants had ever been found in such old rock. No. Only reptile fossils were found in this kind of rock.

Gideon was puzzled. No reptile that he knew about chewed its food. Reptiles gulped their food. So why was this big tooth all worn down? It was a mystery.

Could the tooth have belonged to some gigantic animal that no longer lived on earth? Could the animal have been something like a reptile but different, too?

Gideon went back to the road where Mary Ann had found the tooth. He dug around and found more teeth and some bones.

He took the teeth and bones to a museum in London. At the museum there were skeletons of all kind of animals. Gideon tried to find something that looked like his bones and big, flat teeth. But he found nothing.

Other scientists were studying at the museum too. Gideon showed one of the big stone teeth to another scientist. This scientist was studying iguanas. An iguana is a five-foot-long lizard that lives in South America. The scientist told Gideon that the fossil tooth looked like an iguana tooth.

When Gideon saw an iguana tooth, he was amazed! It did look very much like the mysterious fossil tooth. Only the fossil tooth was much, much bigger.

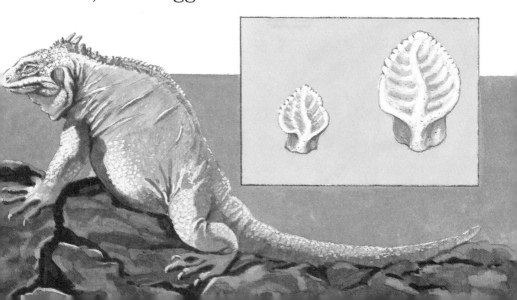

Now Gideon believed the fossil tooth belonged to an animal that looked like a huge, sixty-foot-long iguana! He named his creature *Iguanodon* (i-GWA-nuh-don). That means "iguana tooth."

Gideon did not have a whole Iguanodon skeleton. But he tried to figure out what Iguanodon looked like from the bones and teeth he did have. He thought the bones showed that the creature had walked on all four legs. He thought a pointed bone was a horn. He drew Iguanodon with a horn on its nose.

Years later a complete Iguanodon skeleton was found. It showed that Iguanodon was really only about thirty feet long. It showed that Iguanodon walked on its hind feet. And the horn on its nose was really a spiked weapon on Iguanodon's "thumb"!

The top picture shows what Gideon thought an Iguanodon looked like. The bottom picture shows what an Iguanodon really looked like.

Gideon Mantell made some mistakes. But he did something very important. He wrote a paper for scientists. He said that long ago, before there were any people, huge reptiles lived on earth.

This time nobody was put in prison. People were excited by Gideon's ideas. Now the world couldn't wait to discover more about these huge reptiles.

Soon the fossils of other extinct reptiles were discovered. The fossils showed that they were creatures like modern reptiles in some ways. But in other ways they were very different. For one thing, modern reptiles, such as crocodiles and lizards, have legs that stick out from the sides of their bodies. When they move, their stomachs are low to the ground. But fossils of leg bones showed that the extinct creatures stood with their feet *under* their bodies instead of splayed out to the sides. This was a better way of walking. They did not crawl or slither like modern reptiles.

In 1842 a scientist named Sir Richard Owen decided that these creatures needed a name of their own. In Greek, *deinos* means "terrible" and *sauros* means "lizard." So Owen called these creatures Dinosauria. Today we call them dinosaurs.

3
Here Come
the Dinosaur Hunters!

English dinosaur hunters discovered many new kinds of dinosaurs. Their discoveries made newspaper headlines. People wanted to know everything about these giant creatures.

Artists painted pictures of what they thought dinosaurs looked like. Sculptors built life-size dinosaur statues.

For New Year's Eve in 1853 a scientist sent out invitations to other scientists. When the guests came to the party, they found a table set for twenty-two people *inside* the body of an almost-finished statue of an Iguanodon!

Word of the giant fossil bones spread quickly. By the 1850s dinosaur fever hit America, too. At this time beds for the new railroads were being dug out west. Prospectors were digging for gold in California and Colorado. With so much digging going on, new fossils were uncovered all the time. The western United States was a dinosaur hunter's dream.

Like cowboys, early dinosaur hunters in America were rugged and loved adventure. They carried chisels and rock hammers. They also carried rifles and bowie knives. The West was a wild and dangerous place.

Dinosaur hunters had to live off the land. They had to know where to find water in a desert. They drove stubborn pack mules and clumsy wagons.

Dinosaur hunters called the place where they were working a "dig." They had to figure out how to get huge bones out of solid rock with just picks, shovels, and ropes. When the bones were dug out, dinosaur hunters wrapped them in cloth. They put them in their wagons or on the backs of their mules. Then they headed for the nearest railroad. They shipped the bones back east to bone collectors and museums.

Two of the most famous dinosaur bone collectors were Othniel Marsh of Connecticut and Edward Cope of Pennsylvania. These two paleontologists started out as friends. But soon they became enemies. Each one wanted *all* the dinosaur bones for himself!

In the 1870s, both men headed west. Marsh set up a dig at Como Bluff, Wyoming. Cope went to Como Bluff too. But Marsh would not let him near his dig. So Cope secretly hired one of Marsh's workers. He had the worker take him to Marsh's dig. He looked around. Then he wrote an article about what he had seen. He wrote as if the bones were *his* discovery!

Marsh told his workers to dig out all the bones they could. Then he told them to smash the rest. He did not want Cope to find any more bones from *his* dig!

Other scientists were ashamed of the way Cope and Marsh fought. They thought it gave

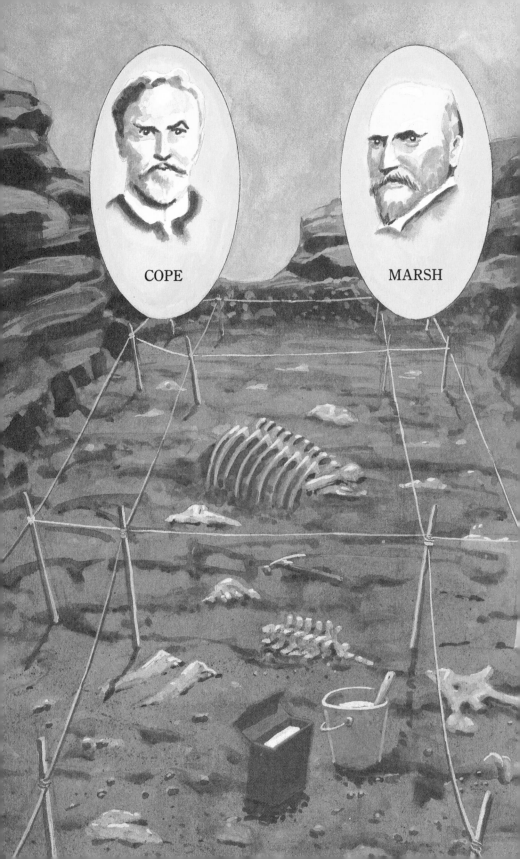

COPE

MARSH

paleontology a bad name. But they had to admit one thing. The war between Cope and Marsh led to tons and *tons* of dinosaur bones being dug up! Marsh alone found more than eighty different types of dinosaurs! He was the first to find Brontosaurus, Stegosaurus (steg-uh-SAWR-us), and Triceratops (try-SER-uh-tops). If you visit Yale University's Peabody Museum or the National Museum in Washington, D.C., you can see Marsh's dinosaurs.

If you go to the American Museum of Natural History in New York City, you can see many of Cope's dinosaurs.

But lots of the bones they found are not on display. They are in museum storerooms and basements. Scientists today still have not finished sorting through all the bones Cope and Marsh dug up over a hundred years ago!

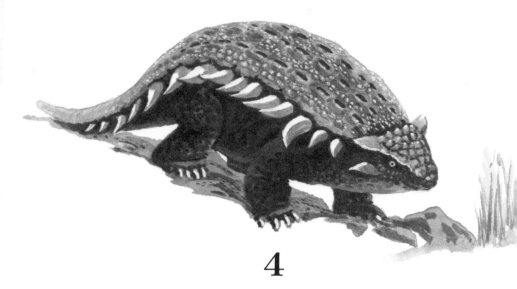

4

Dinosaur Jim's Giants

In many ways dinosaur hunting today is very different from the way it was a hundred years ago. Today's dinosaur hunters have modern tools. They drive trucks instead of mule wagons. But the thrill of finding dinosaur bones hasn't changed. And neither has the long, hard work.

When dinosaur hunters find a place to dig, they make camp. Then they build a wooden roof over the spot where they will dig. The roof protects the fossils that are exposed in the digging. It protects the dinosaur hunters, too.

On most digs the layer of rock above the bones is bulldozed. Then the rock just above the bones is broken up with jackhammers. Next power chisels are used to reach the bones. But dinosaur hunters have to be careful. The bones they hunt are brittle. One wrong move can shatter even a huge dinosaur bone!

Sometimes dinosaur hunters will dig out a big chunk of rock with fossilized bones in it. They do not chip away the rock around the bones. The rock is left around the fossils to protect them. The whole rock is packed in a crate and sent to a museum.

Other times bones are taken out of the rock. But dinosaur hunters do not rush. First a photographer takes a picture of the bones just as they are in the ground. Sometimes an artist will make drawings too. Then each bone is numbered. All this work will help later, when a skeleton is put together again in a museum laboratory.

Next dinosaur hunters pour shellac on each bone as it lies cradled in the rock. The shellac hardens the bones. When the shellac is dry, the bone can be taken out of the rock without breaking.

Little bones can be wrapped in tissue paper and packed in boxes. But bigger bones need more protection. They are first wrapped with tissue paper. Then burlap strips are soaked in wet plaster. The strips are wrapped

around the bone. The tissue paper keeps the plaster from sticking to the bones. The plaster dries into a hard cast just like doctors make for broken bones. Casts protect the big bones while they are being shipped.

Really big dinosaur bones used to be really big problems for dinosaur hunters. They could not lift giant bones out of the ground with just ropes and pulleys. But dinosaur hunters today can use powerful winches to haul out huge bones. Now they can hunt bigger dinosaurs than ever before. And when it comes to finding BIG dinosaurs, nobody is better than Dinosaur Jim.

Dinosaur Jim is like a master spy. He has a network of spies helping him. A shepherd may write Dinosaur Jim a note. He may say he has seen a big bone sticking out of a rock. A quarry digger may phone him. He may say he has dug up a giant skull. A miner may tell Dinosaur Jim of a huge backbone he has uncovered while digging for coal. Dinosaur Jim will check out all these leads.

Dinosaur Jim knows that another good place to hunt for big dinosaurs is in museums! Once, in a museum storeroom, Dinosaur Jim came across the biggest arm bone of a dinosaur he had ever seen. The bone had been dug up in Colorado. Were there any more of the big dinosaur's bones buried in the same place? Dinosaur Jim went to Colorado to find out.

Dinosaur Jim started digging. His hunch was right! He dug up a skeleton of the largest dinosaur ever found! It was related to the eighty-ton Brachiosaurus (bray-kee-uh-SAWR-

us). Until Dinosaur Jim's discovery Brachiosaurus was the largest known dinosaur. But
Dinosaur Jim was sure this new dinosaur was
even bigger. That's why he named it Supersaurus (soup-er-SAWR-us)!

Seven years later, deeper down in this very same spot, Dinosaur Jim dug up another huge bone. It was a shoulder blade. Supersaurus's shoulder blade was eight feet long. This new shoulder blade was ten inches longer! It was from an even *bigger* kind of dinosaur! Dinosaur Jim made his best guess about how much bigger the new dinosaur was. He thinks it weighed one hundred tons! He thinks its leg bones must have been twenty feet tall! This dinosaur was big *beyond* anyone's imagination. Dinosaur Jim named it Ultrasaurus (ul-tra-SAWR-us). That's because *ultra* means "beyond."

Maybe Dinosaur Jim will dig up an even bigger dinosaur someday. But right now Dinosaur Jim wants to study fossils of the very last dinosaurs on earth. He hopes they might someday tell him why all the dinosaurs disappeared.

5

Stories Bones Tell

Digging up dinosaurs often takes months of hard work. Once out of the ground the bones are shipped to museum laboratories. In the labs scientists begin to work with the bones. And their work can take years.

First the dinosaur fossils are unpacked. Plaster casts are cut away. Tissue paper is unwrapped. Then different experts study the bones.

Geologists (jee-OL-uh-jists) study rocks. They study the rock that surrounds fossil bones. They know that rocks contain chemicals, such as uranium. Uranium slowly changes to lead. A rock's age can be told from the amount of lead in it compared to the amount of uranium. The more lead in a rock, the older the rock is.

The oldest dinosaur bones have been found in rock 205 million years old. These skeletons show that dinosaurs were small creatures then. In rock that is from 190 to 135 million years old, skeletons of giant dinosaurs are found. In rock from 135 million to 65 million years old, geologists find many different kinds of dinosaurs. It was during this time that dinosaurs ruled the earth.

The rock surrounding a fossil can tell more than just a dinosaur's age. Are there plant fossils in the rock? They may be clues to what dinosaurs ate. Is the rock from a riverbed? This may be a clue to where dinosaurs lived.

Paleontologists also study the rock. First

they look at photographs from the digs. The way bones are arranged in rock can tell a story.

Many skeletons of a small, birdlike dinosaur called Coelophysis (see-lo-FIE-sis) were found together in New Mexico. This led paleontologists to think Coelophysis may have traveled in herds.

Eventually all the rock around fossils is chipped away. Now paleontologists can work on the fossils themselves. They gather all the bones that they think may be from the same dinosaur. They put the bones on a large, box-like table filled with sand. The sand keeps the bones from rolling around. Then they try to put the bones together like a huge skeleton jigsaw puzzle.

Once the skeleton is put together, paleontologists look for clues. What do the bones tell about the dinosaur they came from?

Are a dinosaur's front legs much shorter than its back legs? It probably walked on its hind legs, like Tyrannosaurus (tie-ran-uh-SAWR-us) rex.

Does it have strong leg bones of about equal size? Then it probably walked on all fours, like Brachiosaurus.

Paleontologists look for any odd marks on bones. Once, a team of paleontologists was studying a skeleton of a Brontosaurus with a piece of its spine missing. The paleontologists looked at the spine closely. There were tooth marks on the bones. The spine had been bitten off! Not far from where the Brontosaurus skeleton was found was an Allosaurus (al-uh-SAWR-us) skull. The paleontologists took the skull. They opened its jaws. They put it next to the Brontosaurus spine. The tooth marks on the Brontosaurus spine matched the Allosaurus teeth perfectly!

Paleontologists find many answers by

studying fossils. But there are always more questions. For example, did the Allosaurus kill the Brontosaurus? Or was it feeding off an already dead animal?

Bones aren't the only storytellers. Fossil footprints can show what a certain dinosaur was doing on a certain day millions of years ago. In Texas some big Brontosaurus footprints were found in a riverbed. Suddenly Allosaurus tracks appear in the mud! Allosaurus was chasing Brontosaurus! The footprints go on. And then they stop. Did Allosaurus catch its prey? Or did Brontosaurus escape? So far, no one has been able to tell.

Triceratops footprints have been found in a circle. In the middle of the circle scientists saw smaller Triceratops prints. Were the Triceratops under attack? Did the adults form a circle around their young to protect them? It looks that way.

Most often fossils that are found belonged to adult dinosaurs. Their bones were big and

heavy. Their teeth were large. They were more likely to become preserved as fossils than tiny bones or teeth, or delicate eggs.

But sometimes fossils of dinosaur eggs do turn up. The eggs of the largest dinosaurs are about the size of basketballs. When the dinosaur babies were born, they were smaller than human babies!

Some fossilized dinosaur nests have been found too. One was discovered in Montana in 1978. The nest was seven feet across and three feet deep. Other nests were around it. They all belonged to a kind of small, duck-billed dinosaur.

Dinosaur hunters had always thought dinosaurs behaved like most reptiles living now. After modern reptiles lay their eggs, they hide or bury them. Then they leave. They never see their young. But the dinosaur nests told a different story.

Eggs were found in one nest. And so were fifteen skeletons of older babies. The older babies were three feet long.

Modern reptile babies hatch on their own. They do not stay in the nest. Their mothers are not around to feed them. So they must go off right away in search of food.

But these duck-billed babies were still in their nest. And their teeth showed that they had been eating plants for some time. How did they get their food? Most likely their mother brought it to the nest. This means that she was taking care of them!

This dinosaur was named Maiasaura (my-uh-SAWR-uh), or "good mother reptile."

Dinosaur hunters have found many amazing fossils. So far, more than 250 different kinds of dinosaurs have been dug out of the ground. But some paleontologists think that once more than five thousand kinds of dinosaurs roamed the earth! That would mean dinosaur hunters still have a lot of digging to do!